A Trout

By

Farhan Bhatti

Intro:

Some of these stories may be true, from work related to old assignments or something I pulled out of my head. I want to thank everyone who encouraged me to finish writing this book as without them, this book would have never been published. Relax and put the kettle on before reading this as I guarantee you wont want to put this down.

With front cover design from Canva

"You cannot make a man smile if a man does not feel like smiling, only when they feel like smiling will they truly smile"

Contents

The Viscount of Chelsea

It was January 25th, 1888, raining heavily with fog covering the whole of London England, in high gate cemetery Viscount Chelsea II had just buried his late wife Madison aged 42

"Oh, my wife, why must thee have had died so young thee had yet so much to live for" mourning his eyes out. The widower Viscount now gazed upon his trusted servant Diablo who also grew up with his wife Madison when they were children playing in her father's foreign exotic garden.

"Diablo as my trusted servant and friend since childhood I am sending you on a journey to bring back my two sons Arelius and Octavzio back to the Chelsea residents"

"As you wish my dear friend" replied Diablo with rain drops rolling off his face along with tears of sorrow walking off into the distance in a separate carriage

Arelius and Octavzio two brothers also known as the two sons of Viscount Chelsea II, both boys were sent to St George boarding school in oxford to learn the ways to fight when it comes to battle and to be gentleman for when they must takeover for their father. As the matron came into the boys' room she handed them both the sad news of the passing of their mother, both boys started weeping and were sad to leave their new friends at the boarding school and were escorted by a recognisable face, diablo.

"You both have grown last I saw u both was the same length of the carriage wheel" smiled Diablo while reading his newspaper

"And you still read books or newspapers Diablo" replied Octavzio sarcastically

"They provide you with knowledge but mostly just to pass the time; we're here now anyway a lot of stuff has changed since you both were last here. Aforesaid diablo while smiling getting out of the carriage.

As they approached the Chelsea mansion the young masters were being greeted and welcomed back by all the Viscount Chelsea members, family, servants, maids and advisors. But most of all their nanny Marianne who was also their half-blood sister which no one else but their mother knew and grew her up in secret.

"Welcome home I've missed you both so much, it feels as if I've not seen you both in centuries" shouted Marianne in joy of being reunited with the two young masters.

"Ah boys there you are I've been looking for you both and would like to introduce thee to your soon to be new mother and my current mistress Mimi" Aforesaid the boys' father.

Both young masters stood there in silence and decided to walk away with their nanny into the mansion to unpack their belongings.

"Don't worry my sweet they will get used to you once you and the boys have got to know each other better." Whispered the Viscount as they walked into the mansion with their arms linked as one.

It was now nightfall everyone in the Chelsea household was now asleep but the two young masters Arelius and Octavzio were still awake telling each other ghost stories their mother used to tell them while by the fire in their chambers. Knock knock, someone was at the door. It was

Mimi their father's mistress coming into the room and shutting the door behind.

"I thought I should just make sure you boys had everything you need and get to know thee more before I marry your father 3 weeks from now. Said Mimi

"I like to play a lot of games but since we have been away for quite a while, I don't know what some of the new things children do now" replied Arelius rubbing his eyes.

"Well." said Octavzio.

Although before he could answer they could hear a large screaming noise coming from down the hall.

AHHHHHHH!!!!

The three of them put on their night gowns and rushed down the stairs to see what all the commission was. The head maid was unconscious, lying above them was the body of their grandfather Viscount of Chelsea I with his head separated on a spike with a note attached. If you do not give up the Viscount of Chelsea name and your lands then more deaths will follow.

Another younger maid came rushing into the main hall and gave the old head maid a glass of cold water to wake her up, all the head maid could say once she awoke was "IT IS COMING" and taken back to her room. Two other servants came and gathered the spike and body away from the mansion to the nearest church. Slowly one by one everyone went back to their chambers or was helping to clean up the mess. Arelius and Octavzio went back to their room in shock not knowing what to do.

"What if we are next" whispered Arelius in shock

"Don't be silly we have guards, no one would harm us, now let's get some sleep" replied Octavzio holding back all emotions.

A few hours later a weird noise could be heard from the boys' room. Boys' come towards the light. Both sat up in their beds and looked at each other.

"Are thee playing a joke on me Octavzio? Shouted Arelius whipping his eyes.

"No but are you pranking me? Replied Octavzio also wiping his eyes.

"

Both were now looking at each other confused to what was going on, behind their mirror a strange light was coming through.

"What do you think the light is?" said Arelius

"I don't know but there is only one way to find out".

Both put on their slippers and nightgowns, pushing the heavy mirror to the side to reveal a hidden passage. Octavzio walked in first followed by Arelius wiping all the huge spider webs that came in their way, they came across many dead bodies and rats which were either rotting or living in the tunnel.

"Go through these doors but all senses will be taken but your eyes and sound" One door led them to a back tunnel going past their father's chambers while he was with his mistress, but the boys were determined and carried on walking. They finally came to a stop and the voice guiding them through was starting to sound familiar.

"Once you have entered the room pour the liquid from the candle on the floor to enlighten the room and all shall be revealed".

Arelius picked up the candle on the ancient dusty table and once some of the wax was melting he poured it onto the floor, the room was lit on fire for a few seconds not harming them and lead a trail of fire to a bigger mirror to what they would not normally see. In the mirror was two figures, they knew straight away who they were it was their mother and Grandfather. The boys were felt with happiness and tears could be seen rolling down their face as they had been granted a second chance to see their mother and other family members who had died with their own eyes.

"My dear boys the one who had killed us both was............ but before she could answer their nanny came into the room, the ghostly figures and fire had disappeared within a blink.

"What are you boys doing here you're not supposed to be here" whispered Marianne

"We were told to come here and saw our mother" replied both.

"Don't be silly both of you, come along now back to bed with the both of you. They closed the door behind and walked back to their chambers to sleep for the remaining time left until they had to wake up early for their grandfather's funeral.

It was now morning the birds were tweeting the atmosphere was cold and raining just like their mother's funeral, they buried their grandfather in the Chelsea mausoleum and greeted all those who came to the funeral service, that same day they had their fathers wedding to their new stepmother Mimi. A note had then arrived delivered from Diablo which was signed by their father to come back to the mansion immediately. They were escorted by Diablo to the nearest carriage the boys' and their nanny were taken back home.

As soon as they had reached the mansion, they had rushed out the carriage and into their father's chambers, he could not be seen in sight.

"Where could father be?" said the young masters.

Footsteps could be heard coming down the corridor the three of them waited in front of the table, as the doorknob was turning to open the door their father came into the room but suddenly, they were ambushed. 10 men with guns in their hands appeared out of nowhere with their faces covered with masks. Their father tried to break free and save the 3 of them but was killed in the process, they were in shock and given sleeping gas until they were unconscious to be taken into a carriage at a secret location.

Splash!!!

Buckets of water was thrown on to them to wake them up from their deep sleep, to reveal they were in separate steel prisons locked up and chained to the wall. The masked man who was standing in the middle of the room was now walking towards their cages.

"I've planned this ever since the beginning, but do you know who I am?" said the mysterious man in a deep voice. The door behind him opened, Mimi had come in unharmed or in chains. What was going on the 3 of them thought?

"Who are you?" shouted Marianne

"Who am I, why it's me Diablo" he replied pulling off his mask. The other men from behind came forward took away their chains and started to punch and kick the nanny and the two boys with Mimi pulling Marianne's hair.

"I was promised even before you two were born to be married to your mother but as we got older she found someone else, your father whom I've served for many years and been like a brother to." Replied Diablo smiling

"We trusted you and this is what you do, did you kill grandfather?" replied Arelius in pain.

"I was actually the one who killed him I hired an assassin to kill him before he knew the truth" replied Mimi walking up to Diablo and being by his side.

"Now to get rid of you 3 before anyone else finds out about this starting with Arelius and Octavzio" replied Diablo

"NO!!!" Marianne got on to her two feet and charged towards Diablo punching him with all the energy she had left before the other men and Mimi grabbed her.

"Just for that kill the boys and spread their bodies across London, as for you take her to my chambers and lock her up".

Without hesitation and any questions, they did as Diablo had requested, the look of fear on their faces was something no man, women or child could ever forget with the weeping of tears and blood that was splashed everywhere. Spreading the evidence across London and dumping some of it in the river Thames was hard work with policeman and civilians at night wondering around the streets of London. Marianne was taken to Diablos chambers and sadly raped to death. As Mimi had married their father the previous viscount, she gained all rights of Chelsea and married Diablo to become the new viscount of Chelsea and having 5 children. A few years later Diablo discovered a letter in his study addressed to him the same date Madison had died, revealing Marianne was his daughter but was kept away in secret, all he could think about was, what had he done.

Tragedy of the Twins

Glass fell like hail stones, joining the snow of winter. People ran screaming for their lives. It was so early in the morning and so many innocent people had already died. Smoke billowed from the building, hot as a volcano, like a dragon breathing its anger towards the city. This is how the tragedy happened on that day; this is how the real story behind those atrocious events.

In a café, I was getting my breakfast, so cold and hungry and waiting to be served my food: a nice hot rich coffee and a bagel. My stomach was crying for food. But then I had got a phone call about an emergency, an explosion at the Twin Towers. A tragedy at the heart of the city. I dropped my breakfast and ran out of the café. Raced to the fire department in my red-hot jaguar. My girlfriend worked in the North Tower and the only thing on my mind was to save her; her and the other citizens. Coffee had splashed on to my new shirt and tie: it left a stain like a detonated bomb.

I arrived at the scene of the disaster. The Twin Towers were in ruin, burning, blazing. People were screaming and shouting and running in panic. The air tasted of fear. People had no clue what was going on. A plane had slammed into the building. Fire erupted from the gaping wound left behind. Joining the other fire-fighters, I ran towards the building. I ran past three policemen, and heard them whispering, "Has the eagle from the south hit yet?" I had no clue what they meant by that and carried on running.

The fire from the building was so violent that no one dared go into the building. Its flames were death to anyone who came near it. The fire had spread from the very top floor, crawling its way down slowly like a snake stalking its prey in an autumnal jungle. As the fire reached the ground floor, it exhaled one final breath and destroyed anything in its way that remained. The doors of the building were blown, and the windows shattered into innumerable shards.

Charging into the building, I ran against the flow, dodging others who were running for their lives to get to safety. A few seconds later, I realised what the policemen had meant by, "has the eagle from the south hit yet?" They were behind the attack.

Shouting my girlfriend's name, I searched frantically for her.

I was not fast enough.

The roof shook and collapsed on top of me.

I awoke to droplets of water falling onto my face. I moved my head to the side, looking for hope, for an escape. Instead, I saw my girlfriend on the floor, unconscious. I struggled to my feet, pushing the rubble out of my way. I shook her to wake her up. On the third attempt she woke up, I helped her to rise, and we walked to the exit slowly. Behind us, the building gloomed and sighed, slowly and dying.

I discovered later that another plane had hit the building. The floors above us collapsed. We were barricaded from one another. I could hear her feeble cries nearby. I tired breaking the wall with my own fists to make a tiny gap to get to her. It was futile. More of the building was now breaking apart but I was not leaving her behind. Spotting an emergency axe on the floor, I grabbed it. I smashed a gap in the rubble for a hole for her to crawl through. The remaining part of the roof was about to collapse. I grabbed her outstretched arm.

The celling groaned. I pulled. Just as the concreate fell, I pulled her free and we escaped.

Through fire and smoke, death and despair, clothing to each other, we ran stumbled out of the dying building and into the brilliant sunlight. We survived but how many innocent victims that day did not?

Out of the blue

Am I believing breathing watching in the white building

My nerves and eyes sagging flagging falling

Anyone watching in fact I am behind the white shirt waving waving.

In the distant clouds burning when you are appalling appalling am I not worth saving?

Here I surrender watching you as I disappear out of the blue.

Pure forest

On this day, every year in the forest of pure women, a woman on an ancient, decorated boat, looking for her love who she never got to meet as their love was forbidden with both lovers being from different parts of the forest can be seen.

Their love forbidden as they came from different classes during the French revolution, her a Duchess and him the son of a clock maker. They would always play with each other when they were kids and one day that was when they realised they were supposed to be together but because of the revolution poor turned against rich, rich turned against poor.

Annabelle was her name as sweet and delicate as the river Nile her hair was gingery red which moved like fire in the wind, the boat you could always see her in she got from the person who loved her like the white cold snow you would wake up to in winter when you were a young child with the money he had earned as it reminded him of her glazed eyes. She would always like to paint and read books with Thomas, that is why she would like to act in the city and look at all the different performances that would be on to see what they could do together someday.

The boat is what kept the two lovers together as it represents their love for each other, like Christmas day of opening your wrapped present from the person who cares about you. And if you still have not figured it out I was the lover who never got to meet her before the revolution had started.

The Painter

1967 Paris, France Madam Robbie is having her house painted from head to toe she hired every artist and decorator in Paris and beyond just to paint her house inside and out but didn't like the work of any of them, until one day a man nor artist or decorator named Francis Blanc a local baker married with 4 children who lived above the bakery overheard from a customer about Madam Robbie about how she was looking for an artist or decorator to paint her house. Francis had found this to be interesting and decided to approach her for the job. So, every day when Francis had finished his job he would practice painting in different textures and colours, until the actual day he would start.

"Your work is horrible and outdated nor are you an artist, leave my home now in one piece before I change my mind"

Francis had left Madam Robbie home immediately depressed and grey. Until he came across an old man wearing a dusty old black, he looked very weird like one of those people who are poor living in the streets who steal for a living.

"Take this book and follow each instruction this book provides to achieve all your life dreams but be warmed every wish you make will have a consequence" said the mysterious old man.

Francis went home to speak to his wife and children about it and did as the old man had said following each instruction written in the book. The book given by the old man was very hard to read as the language it was written in was very old or written in a different context, the book cover and pages were tearing apart easily as you would just turn the page. 1 cup of ink, 2 boiled eyeballs of both animal and man, fresh herbs pointed towards the south even when a seed.

Whizz!! POP!! BANG!!

Francis had tried everything as written in the book time after time after time, yet it still wouldn't work, he started to think the old man had tricked him and threw the book away until one day his youngest daughter Julia while coming home from selling bread to an old women came across the book outside their bakery shop, she took the book in and hid it away from her older brothers and parents realising the book was the same as the one her father had brought home one night before.

Later that same day before she had gone to bed Julia had grabbed the book from where she had hidden it cutting her hand from the book, reciting, and repeating the exact same actions her father had done a few drops of blood fell from her hand onto the bowl she was casting the spell, in a flash smoke had flooded the room a mysterious figure had come out. In a large black coat, skin cold as ice, hair long and thick and standing very tall you could tell he was not to be messed with.

"What is your name and why have you summoned me"? Said the figure in a deep voice

"My name is Julia and I have summoned you to help my father? She replied

"That is all I needed to hear, I shall help your father by granting you four wishes of your choosing, pick wisely and be careful what you wish for, you may call me the man of many faces". He replied smirking and with that he disappeared.

Julia looked around to see if he were still around but could not find him in sight.

"I wish for my father to be able to paint and rich" Julia said before rubbing her eyes to fall asleep.

"Your wish shall be granted but be warned what might happen may not be what you want it to be" he whispered.

The next morning everyone in the house had awaken and found money in different parts of their little home, they were rich and artwork which was made by their father was up on the walls, everyone was confused why they had so much money but continued as they usual running the bakery and delivering food to elderly customers. Julia knew inside her 2 wishes had come true and she only had 2 remaining so she better uses them wisely. Her father started to perfect his artwork and decorating to then rise up on the challenge set by Madam Rault, he arrived at her house in clothes which were better in quality drawing whatever he could think of Julia was watching from behind the door as the wish was taking place.

Rault was impressed and paid him for his artwork amazed by what he had drawn asking him to return tomorrow to decorate her house. He left her mansion and strolled back to the bakery to tell the family the great news, they were pleased but their son Johnathan had passed away due to an accidental horse carriage crash while on the way home from school, this did not stop them as Francis would avenge his late son's death even if it were to kill him.

That fortnight Julia kept thinking to herself was the death of one of her brothers caused by her wish or just really just an accident, she called out for the man of many faces and asked him, he was getting older and grey simply replying

"I have no control what happens, but you look as if you have another wish to get off your chest"

"I wish for my father to accomplish the decorating job tomorrow" she said

"As you wish but be warned what happens next cannot be reversed through time nor space" and with that the man of many faces had disappeared again into the darkness.

The next morning her father had left the bakery early leaving them breakfast and chores to do while he was away their mother had left during the night and fled France with their uncle to Germany taking nearly all the money promising to return one day to come back for them. Her two remaining brothers were lying on the floor cold and beaten to death they had been robbed. Julia ran for life to find her father to then realise he must of have gone to Madam Rault mansion to start working and rushed to find him pushing and shoving pass people in the streets of Paris.

She finally found him walking into the mansion with different cans of paint and wallpapers for the decorating job, Julia ran towards him but was stopped by the bodyguards of madam Rault. 2 hours inside and outside, top to bottom it took him to paint and decorate the house with sweat dripping off his face by himself with a few others, although it should have taken longer thought madam Rault. Rault still thanked Francis and gave him the reward money as promised and with that he left the mansion to now walk back to the bakery, Julia was released by the servants and rushed towards her father, but it was too late.

He had lost consciousness and fell flat to the ground in the middle of the street not moving or breathing, people rushed to help aid him, but all was futile Julia came and held her father's body.

"I did all of this to help you father" she said crying his lips were moving but no sounds could be heard and with that he fell asleep. The man of many faces now appeared in front of Julia and asked her for the last and final wish.

"I wish not to be alone and be with the rest of my family" she replied, the man of many faces did as she requested and within seconds later she as well had fallen into a deep death sleep. The mysterious man now took his leave and the book which brought him here to find a new master to never be seen again, as for their mother she had committed suicide after hearing the news of their tragic deaths. Some say they still call for him to help or the Blanc family are still able to be seen at their old bakery now a 4-bedroom house.

Prison school

Now I am sure many people have felt like going to secondary school and the atmosphere of the school is like a prison, but what if I told you about my school? The prison schools. The first day of secondary you'll always have to take pictures with your parents or older/younger siblings, who are also attending that school, holding back your tears and emotions for all your old friends you have ever met while in primary who you'll never meet unless crossing paths in public or going the same way. The first day is always important and your parents would probably be worrying more about if you will be ok or not making sure you have packed everything that you may need.

9:00am your first day starts a bit late from when you would normally start but you would get used to it, your parents wait with you on your first day while other years go straight in. Two teachers who you've probably never met before coming out to greet you all the new fresh meat of the school. They joke and laugh with your parents/carers and say

"You're now theirs" taking you all into the school with your parents/carers now waving goodbye reminding you to meet them at the front of the school. Once you made your first step into the school building they welcome you in with open arms but really make you zip your mouth shut and throw away the key, making you line up into your colour ties and assigning you a tutor. Marching one by one you all have been taken to a room with other people the same age as you and are forced to tell each other your names and interests.

After they introduce to you the rules of their site and what they expect, taking you down now to the prison hall where you are now all glued to your seats, doors and exits shut closed. The headmaster/mistress now gives their speech what is expected and welcomes you to their house and games introducing the other teachers or should I say the house security officers. Your forced to put your hands together and clap in rhythm they tell you about their pass students and GCSE results, putting you into a deep sleep to brain wash you without you knowing that once you have got into year 11 to then move on to their post 16 (sixth form) as it's the best in the country when actually it's not.

You now are awakened from your deep sleep forgotten the events of what had happened in that assembly and find yourself with the others in your year in that room, they have finished speaking to you and now dismiss you all to go home with that same assembly hall event happing to you all for the next days over and over again. Many years past you have made and lost many friends and teachers on your journey although you now are in year 11, doing your exams, attending revision sessions, and respecting others. You start to see what they do with the new fresh meat which once used to be you, wondering, confusion, uncertainty did they do that with your year?

GCSE results day you come in with one thing in your mind did I get the grades to move on?

You see your friends and wait with them patiently outside catching up on stuff with a few laughs and giggles. It's now time to make your move into the building which once looked like a prison and still is, lined up in rows by your surname to collect an envelope with your grades the teacher gives you the envelop and you go to one side. Lifting one side of the envelop pulling the flap off to pull out your sheet of grades. Your friends are smiling and crying with joy while you are left on your own two feet with a piece of paper, it never went your way, but you may have just got a couple of GCSEs. Your heart pounding in fear glimpsing an eye on other people's sheet to see what they got, people you know including your friends asking, what did you get?

Afraid, ashamed, depressed only a few words come out of your mouth.

"It's ok" holding back the emotions your feeling, outside and inside the building you can see others in the same or similar pile as you. Teachers walking across the hall to those who have got what they need discussing options for A-levels or BTECS while those who did not ignored and thrown to the side to be abandoned at such young ages no support or teacher to talk to. Going to enrol for sixth form seeing if there is still any hope, looking at your grade sheet and their entry requirements with a pen in their hand, glancing into your eyes which are full of fear, confusion, and sadness to revel they cannot do anything for you giving your place to someone outside the school wall…….. But promise they will get someone to call you, no one does.

Your lost, confused and depressed not knowing what to do or how your parents will react, with only 2 weeks to sort something out. But you're not alone as your family are still there for you, another door has opened you just have to open it, the making of you, proving they are making a mistake of not letting you in. some of your friends may not contact you ever again although you find out they are praising those who passed. For those wondering this story is set on what had happened to me on my GCSE results day and how I felt.

Love cycle

For it was months before valentine's day and a year, little did KT know his girlfriend soon to be wife Nikita was planning a special surprise for their big day. The two lovebirds had been together for three years and met through friends like Rebecca, Junk and many more while at college. All was going to plan, a romantic dinner with candles, drinks, and free music at the fanciest restaurant in the greatest town of Southwark booked for two at McDonalds. Until one day KT had found his beautiful young girlfriend had been cheating on him with Robert. His heart was broken, the girl of his dreams had stabbed him in the back, he did not confront them and brushed it off as if it had never happened. They got married and lived together for a year, but behind his back she still desired Robert. A year had passed and KT birthday was coming up, the pain kept poking him in the heart that he finally snapped, he was going to kill her before the bong of midnight.

It was the day of his birthday and soon in 15 hours KT would be able to murder Nikita. If he wanted to kill her it would need to happen precisely at the struck of 12 not a second before or after and happen where no one would see it happen, in their home. He popped down to the local shops and markets to gather the goods he would need, placing all the traps around the house and setting one or two in each room positioned at an angle Nikita would not see it coming. After a while kt received a text message from Nikita

"Meet me at Junks restaurant home of glorious foods and wonders at 7, I've got a surprise".

He wondered why Nikita would send him a message to meet at Junks restaurant, maybe she was finally going to confess, or she was going to kill him.

KT got dressed and wore a suit for the occasion imagining he was James Bond driving in his Jaguar down to Junk's restaurant. As he arrived, she was waiting outside for him, and they walked inside. The restaurant had 5 floors which could fit one football pitch for each floor, round tables shaped like circles and three candles all different candles. By time they got their seats it was already 8 he only had a few hours to kill her.

"Happy Birthday, and the surprise was his sister Michelle, Robert and a few others were going to meet them" said Nikita.

He was astonished, how would he get away and drag Mimi back to the house and finally dispose of Robert.

KT tried his hardest to look surprised to the news Nikita gave him, so he gave her a little smile as if he were constipated but Nikita took no notice, Michelle and Robert came along slowly afterwards. He tried his hardest not to look angry at Robert or cause a scene, so he shook his hand and hugged him, after a while they played a few games, drank, ate meal after meal of Junks restaurant food until they were stuffed like roast chicken, and they could see it was almost 10:40.

"We should head back" said Nikita.

They agreed, paying for their meal and left Junk's restaurant in their car, Nikita drove. They were taking a different route to the house, which KT was not familiar with in the dark, Nikita asked him to wear a blind fold made from her panties or it would ruin the surprise, he started to think of all the different possible surprises it could be, maybe it was a gift to show she was sorry, a new car, something from Victoria secret or maybe she knew already that he was going to kill her?

They arrived at the house and Michelle helped KT get out of the car but made him slip and fall on top of her and Nikita. Robert helped them up, guiding KT to the house and removed his blind fold, KT pulled out a knife from his pocket and click the lights turned on for everyone to shout.

"SURPRISE"!!!

His cousin Rebecca was bringing the birthday cake over and put the knife through the cake as if nothing had happened,

"And the final surprise is I'm pregnant" said Nikita.

Everyone burst into tears of happiness to hear the good news Nikita was pregnant and going to have their first baby. KT was stunned. He could not move an inch. If he were to kill Nikita, he will also then be killing his own child. As time went on it slowly approached 12 the guest were leaving the house, thanking them for the KT surprise birthday party, he had to get Nikita away from the ground floor rooms otherwise all the traps he had set out will be released and kill her and the baby. KT looked for Nikita rushing room to room in search for Nikita, he finally found her upstairs waiting on their bed in a Victoria secret lingerie.

Killer could hear the traps going off during the night, so he held himself tightly against Nikita moving in closer and made loud wind sounds to cover the trap noises. Once it was morning, he rushed downstairs to put the washing machine on, take the rubbish out and made breakfast for himself and Nikita. He then remembered that the traps were going off during the romantic night with Nikita so he rushed to all the rooms to clean up the mess only to find that Robert was on the couch who had a bullet and trap dart through his chest, he appeared dead and his body cold as ice, most of the blood was soaked into the couch, cushions and floor and Nikita could come down at any moment.

Robert was possibly dead, and footsteps could be heard moving around upstairs and going into the shower, KT needed to hide the body and somehow remove the blood before Nikita could find the body and scream the house down. He tried hiding the body behind the sofa in the sofa and underneath but no matter how hard he tried one part of Robert possible dead body would stick out, he tried behind the TV, but Robert was too round and fat, probably by the food from Junks greasy restaurant, Killer even tried behind the living room blinds but you would then see his feet or people outside would see his melons. He then went on to try flush Robert down the toilet, but he was too big and would cause the toilet to overflow, throwing him out the window, but the old couple Geri and J would see the body and so would the others on the street.

KT had no other choice he would have to put Robert's body in the spare room below the stairs next to the boiler. Once Nikita was finished taking her shower, she put her bath robe on and walked downstairs still in her Victoria secret lingerie if KT wanted to carry on from last night. KT cheeks were blushing red like strawberries, Nikita could see he was enjoying it, but he turned down the offer and made her breakfast instead. Michelle came over after she could smell the delicious food being made from miles away with Steve and Cousin Rebecca. They discussed how long she had known she was pregnant, that is when he found out that the child surely must be his and which room was going to be the babies, they finally came to the conclusion that the spare room next to theirs would be the baby's room once it was born.

"Let me just get my clothes" said Nikita attempting to hide her lingerie from Steve peeping eyes.

"Don't worry about it, I'll get them for you, where did you leave them last?" asked Michelle

"In the spare room underneath the stairs" said Nikita.

Steve tried his best to see what Nikita was wearing underneath the robe, but Nikita would have to move her hand all over her body to stop him. That is when KT realised he left Robert's body there.

"I'll go with you to find them" said KT.

They walked off to the spare room together. KT picked up the knife left on the table and placed his sleeve in case something was to happen, Michelle found the room and opened the door.

As Michelle opened the door, KT pulled out the knife and held it in his hand pocket in case she saw the body, and he would need to dispose of her. As the door opened even wider Michelle screamed like a firework KT pulled the knife out and was about to strike until he realised, she was screaming to have been startled by coming across Nikita's toys and clothes. KT was relieved and shoved the knife back down his pocket, Michelle took the clothes and toys back to Nikita, but Killer was shocked to find Robert's body had vanished, could he have been alive?

KT shut the door and scanned the room to see if the body must have fallen out when closing the door earlier. The body was nowhere in sight, KT shut the door and continued to search for Robert.

"It's no luck he must be still alive" KT mumbled to himself.

KT then walked back to Nikita and the rest, dashing the knife underneath the pile of coats away from clear sight. While walking back KT could see Michelle was helping Nikita to get dressed and the blue haired ninja pervert Steve was trying to get a glimpse of the action, but KT took no notice, it was only until later he could see droplets of blood going through the hallway and smudge across parts of the walls, that he decided to investigate. In the middle of the stairs around the corner Robert was slouching trying to make his way upstairs into the toilet, KT tip toed back to fetch the knife and end Robert from behind and was ready to pounce but Nikita and Steve came from the other side asking

"What was going on?"

KT hesitated to answer and could not finish off the work, so he quickly took off his shirt and placed it on top of Robert.

"I was just taking out the trash and putting the laundry away" said KT.

He pulled all of Roberts's parts together and stuffed them into his shirt leaving room for him to breath and took him upstairs into the master bedroom. Nikita was suspicious but Steve the blue haired ninja pervert would keep her entertained only meaning Michelle would slap him on the ass or face a few times to behave but he was intrigued to see what was underneath and what Nikita was wearing. Meanwhile KT was helping Robert to clean his body using Jerry's research toilet paper, once KT was done helping to clean he pushed Robert causing him to fall backwards and smash his head hard against the bar of soap.

As soon as he was out cold KT dragged Robert back down into the basement and tied him up in Chanel's Ozz house ropes, masks, and chains, so he would not be able to escape or scream loudly for anyone to hear. As his face was covered KT could torture him as much as he wanted until he got valuable information and had no use of him anymore, but KT decided to keep him locked until he rotted himself to death.

KT strike one blow to his nuts and bolts causing Robert to be in agony, but Nikita could be heard calling for him, he would have to finish the job later and see what his pregnant wife needed. Nikita was trying to call Robert as his car was still outside the house. She tried calling for him like a dog, but he wouldn't answer, if only she knew he was just one floor beneath her, she then attempted to ring his second phone for KT to realise he forgot to remove from his back pocket after confiscating it from him.

"That's strange, every time I try to ring Robert your phone goes off as well" said Nikita.

KT looked puzzled and pretended not to know why, Nikita tried again.

"I can hear something below as if it's coming from the basement. She said.

Nikita strolled to the basement door, but KT got in her way.

"Move KT or I'll get Steve to break it down" said Nikita.

He refused to move, Steve tried to push KT to the side, but KT pushed him back, opened the door and walked down the basement stairs to where Robert was, locking the door behind him from the inside. KT rushed as quickly as he could only to find Robert was not there, someone must have freed him or he had escaped through the Chanel ropes, Nikita and Steve then came crashing through the door chasing after KT to see why he was acting so suspicious, only to find he was standing in the basement alone. Steve and Nikita looked puzzled to why he acted in a weird manner only to be by himself. KT looked around the room to see if Robert left any tracks or clues behind to where he might have disappeared to, but nothing could be used to reveal where Robert could have gone.

"I was trying to keep it as a secret, but I was making you a baby cradle and basket for the baby coming." Said KT

Nikita was surprised and felt terrible for demanding to see what was in the basement. They went back upstairs, KT first followed by Nikita and of course the blue haired ninja pervert Steve trying to still catch a glimpse of Nikita from behind with his mini Bruce Frey bicycle camera. Steve shut the door only to find on the ground accompanied by poison with blood pouring out of his damaged body and patches of skin torn into human mash potato, Robert. They rushed to help Robert and rang an ambulance to take him to the hospital, while they waited anxiously Nikita grabbed bandages and anything else she could find ripping her shirt catching the eyes of Steve and ripping his shirt to reveal the frozen limited edition shirt, all Robert could say was do not put me in the same room as the beast.

As Robert fainted mumbling those words, the two paramedics took him into the ambulance and were off to the hospital. While at the hospital waiting for Robert to come out of the operation room Nikita, Steve and Michelle thought to themselves what Robert meant by his last words before sounding like a drunk Irishmen and fainting in Michelle's lap like a princess.

"He was probably drunk" said KT, trying to break the awkward silence and stop them from looking at him oddly.

"He's probably right" said Steve, scrolling through his little camera for all the photos he had taken for his research and man cave.

Robert had finally come out of the operation room asleep, Doctor Grumpy tried his best to fix and restore Robert to his full health, but he would need to stay at the hospital for 2-4 weeks just to ensure his wounds had healed. The three of them were relieved apart from KT who needed to dispose of Robert before he snitches on him, they said their goodbyes and promised to see him again in the morning. The four of them visited Robert daily while he stayed at the hospital as each day passed he became stronger until finally on the third week 4 days before Robert could be discharged, KT was planning on an assassin from

Jesses quick and pay later kill organisation, the 1000 best in the world and cheapest. He instructed the assassin Dank to kill anyone they saw in the room including Robert without being seen and staying in the shadows. KT went with the assassin to show him the room to kill Robert, the assassin took out his silencer gun ready to shoot but sleeping in the curved hospital chair was Nikita.

The hitman was already in the room scouting the area but luckily did not see Nikita as she was underneath her long coat. She was about to wake up and release the loudest yawn you could hear in the hospital, the assassin Dank was spooked by the yawn and started firing shots all over the place, causing KT to come barging into the room and the assassin Dank jumping out the window landing on a fat anchor sitting outside the hospital little garden for patients. Nikita looked around thinking she was crazy hearing gun shots in the hospital room she was in. KT quickly explained it was just the window as it had shattered to millions of tiny snow drops, poking his head out the window to see where the assassin Dank was but he was knocked out by the cold and anchor below with stars in his eyes, KT closed the blinds to stop the cold breeze from effecting the room.

Robert was waking up from his nap and was surprised to see Nikita and KT very early in the morning to visit him, the doctor finally came in to check Robert's wounds, blood pressure etc. and they all came back clear for him to leave the hospital. They helped Robert into the wheelchair taking him downstairs to get discharged and into the car to drive home.

"I'll be back, I just need to make a phone call" said KT.

He was trying to call the assassin Dank to strike again but he refused the job as his hairy pineapple ass was still recovering from the dreadful fall. KT was not impressed throwing his phone to the ground, furiously and crushing it to bits before returning to the car. On the long drive home from the hospital, they saw the blue haired ninja pervert Steve and Michelle, to confirm they should prepare for a surprise return party for Robert, but miles away from home Robert was sitting in the back of the car eyeing KT In a curious way, leaping himself forward for the car to go off course and crash in the middle of nowhere and the beautiful Nikita's water had erupted in the car.

The car had crashed and in the middle of nowhere, the baby was on its way and letting its present known as Nikita was screaming the car down as the pain became stronger by the second as if she had been punched in the gut. KT was unconscious thanks to Robert making them crash in the middle of nowhere but close to the countryside miles away from any building or emergency phone lines. Nikita tried to wake up KT by shaking him viciously but eventually found a way by wetting his pants with her water bottle. Thanks to Robert being at the back of the car and leaping himself forward at his prey he ended up going flying through the car window with blood stained on the glass and ground, KT kicked the car door opened and crawled out towards the bloody faced man in front of him, punching and kicking him until more blood was falling down his face, KT fell backwards onto his back with exhaustion.

"That's for making the car go off course" said KT.

KT had struck one of Roberts nerves. The two of them slowly got up to their feet and were going to fight to death, Nikita continued to scream in agony as her water broke and the baby's head was now visible, she grabbed her phone from underneath her seat and tried to ring an ambulance. Due to the slippery road the car Michelle and Steve were in went flying into the small ford of KT's rented car and caused the two cars to flip over and crash, leaving Nikita and the baby to be trapped inside the two collided cars. Fire spitting out of the cars like a dragon's flamethrower, Robert, Kt and the others rushed to the cars to quickly get them out of the rubble before the fire became unbearable and wild like a crazy bull.

KT and Robert could see Nikita trapped in the metal and it looked as if other car doors had pierced through her skin and possibly through her stomach, they needed to act quickly, and it became a competition between the two men of saving Nikita's life in time as well as saving Steve and Michelle. They got them out in time, but nothing could have been done to help save Nikita as she was still stuck barricaded between the two cars and both of them were trying to pull her from each side like a toy. They pulled and pulled but she would not move as she was trapped, they went further into the car removing her clothes from catching on fire and see if she had any injuries.

Only a few could be seen but it was the babies and Nikita's life which concerned KT the most, they finally got her out as the car roared violently as the fire was starting to melt the insides of the half-backed remains of the cars. Nikita was taken into the ambulance back to the hospital along with the others to ensure they were ok. After a few hours the baby was delivered but Nikita was hurt everywhere on her body due to the crash, they had her on drugs while KT and the others in the room had a look at the new beautiful little baby for Nikita to reveal something in KT's ear, but her sister Gina had come barging in leaving KT unable to find out what Nikita was trying to say.

Nikita's younger sister Gina had come barging into the hospital room to see her new baby nephew,

"Let me see the precious" she shouted.

Her face polished with red blush like a tomato as she saw the baby, leaving KT clueless to what Nikita was trying to tell him. He tried numerous amounts of times to get her attention to ask what she was trying to say but would be distracted by the others in the room and Steve trying to make the baby have blue hair. Once he finally got his turn to ask her, the nurse had come in asking him to leave so Nikita and the baby could sleep and take their medication. As Gina had come to see her sister Nikita, KT offered to let her stay at their house for a few weeks or longer depending how long she was going to stay, this gave KT the perfect plan he would use Gina to find out what Nikita had said, but how would he do it and he would have to keep an eye out for Michelle as well as Cousin Rebecca and Robert.

He treated Gina and helped her unpack her bags, he invited her for dinner at Junks sloppy exotic mouth-watering restaurant, there they had the Junk classic, as they ate KT asked Gina if she would do him a favour of finding out what she was going to tell him, but she laughed drunkenly and replied.

"I know why you really invited me, you've been looking at me differently since I came back to town to see my sister" she said.

Moving her chair closer and placing her hand on top of his and kissing him, they then got back in the car and headed to the guest bedroom. Before KT could resist and tell Gina no, it was all over he had just made the biggest mistake imaginable. He quickly got his clothes back on, but Gina was tempted to keep him in the room by her side. He stayed with his eyes wide opened during the night waiting for Gina to finally pass out asleep, so he could leave the room and forget what had taken place, imagining as if it never happened. He went downstairs put his clothes back on and went for a drive in his car driving through the town, he then thought to pay Nikita a visit as it was 3am in the morning as he turned the car around to drive in the opposite direction his phone began to vibrate. It was Gina.

He switched his phone to silent and concentrated on the silence around him while the phone continued vibrating, missed call after missed call. Eventually he got sick of it and threw the phone out the window and at that exact moment, Robert jumped from behind the driver's seat with a metal chain placing it over KT's neck to strangle him while another came flying from the side causing the car to flip over like a upside down pancake. Robert had hired an assassin Hunter1111 to help in the assistance of getting rid of KT for good after as he tried to dispose of him, the assassin got out of her car and broke the driver car KT was behind to get him out and finish the job, but KT had escaped through the other side and trapped Riley in the front.

He then knocked out the hired assassin and locked her in the hand cuffs he used on Nikita, locking the assassin to the car door handle, escaping the scene with the assassin's rented Jaguar F type. KT was off and hurrying before Robert could wake up, he decided to go back home as it was closer, leaving the hospital for another day or possibly later. As he got to the house Gina was waiting outside in a dressing gown which belonged to Nikita, she looked very surprised to see him and the reason was she had found about KT trying to kill Nikita and Robert.

Gina was sitting outside the house in the cold with a strange book in her hand containing KT's master plan and it was there that he realised she must have read his plan. KT got out of the car and rushed out towards Gina, she got up as quickly as she could and ran inside forgetting to close the door behind her, she attempted to run up the stairs, but killer caught her ankle and dragged her down the stairs. Gina kicked KT in the apple tree rushing pass as he fell to the ground knees first and tried to dial for the police. But KT stopped Gina and explained he was not going to harm her if she was to help him dispose of Robert. Threatened for her life and possibly never seeing those close to her again, Gina agreed to help KT make Robert vanish not for a short while but forever.

Heading to the hospital the next day, they ran into Steve with Nikita playing with his camera as Nikita was coming home, they took her home and helped her get back to her usual routine, KT and Gina were then off in search to find Robert scanning the streets for him and it was at that moment that Gina had muttered aloud by accident the flat he was staying in. KT turned the car furiously and drove extremely fast to the potential location of Robert.

They spotted Robert on the streets and tried to run him over, but he ran away as fast as he could to his flat. KT and Gina chased after him breaking the gate and the wooden front door of the flat, chasing him all the way to the 15 fleet of stairs to his room barging the door repeatedly until it crumbled. The two of them fought like cats and dogs, KT held Robert down placing a plastic bag over his head, strangling him as he struggled to breath, shouting at Gina to slam the door on Robert, stab him and more until he's cold, Gina didn't want to.

"Do it Gina"!!! Shouted KT as Robert was almost free.

Gina slammed the door on Robert's chest numerous times and got the hammer, just to make sure KT took the hammer from Gina and hit Robert a few more times with it.

"Let's get out of here, before we get caught", exclaimed KT. They ran out of the flat and drove away.

KT and Gina had just killed Robert and were now fleeing the scene before the police arrive and arrest them. The blood was all over Gina's clothes and KT hands as they drove away into the distance back to the house using side routes to keep away from the camera and being caught by the police, they needed to get to the house quickly and make sure they were not being followed. They dumped the car outside a park and took any evidence with them burying it deep in their bags or scattering it across the path they were on, walking the rest of the way to Primark and a few other shops to replace their blood covered clothes. Gina ran into Michelle in the ladies changing room and it was there she saw blood on Gina's clothes and droplets of blood smudged on the wall, Michelle was about to scream for help thinking Gina had been hurt and with the men's changing room being next door KT rushed quickly to the other side, pulling the both of them into the nearest vacant changing room and placing a knife over her neck.

"What did you tell her!". Exclaimed KT.

"Nothing, I swear please don't hurt her" pleaded Gina.

He looked at Michelle with his eyes very sharp. Michelle tried to scream for help and tell Gina to run, but KT immediately took out the knife and slit Michelle's throat. Gina ran out of the store with KT chasing after her and bumping into Steve holding all of Michelle's shopping bags from Next, River Island and BHS. Steve asked if he had seen Michelle and told him he last saw her in the ladies changing room and dashed after Gina. Steve walked towards the changing room, waiting patiently for Michelle but other people would just walk in and out, he even tried shouting for her but no reply. Noticing a weird smell coming from one of the rooms, he investigated to see the cause, it was Michelle dead like a headless chicken and straight away called for the police.

By that time KT had caught up to Gina and they both took off to keep low until the heat cooled down, it was tough for him to explain why he was going away for some months but said it was a business trip to Nikita looking after the baby by herself. It was lonely on the roads driving around London, so KT travelled with Gina making them closer and their feeling getting out of control, with more regret piling as the chip on his shoulder grew larger. Once many months had passed and the heat had gone low they returned to Lambeth where Nikita and the baby were, as they came home everything went back to normal or so it seemed when Gina and Nikita were having a meal together it had slipped from her lips that she was pregnant with KT's baby. Nikita was also shocked and claimed to be pregnant again with KT's baby too, Gina did not believe her, and the two sisters started to brawl over the same man they loved.

The 9 month old baby Nikita had earlier was in the other room asleep while the two of them fought their hearts out scratching and crawling at one another, Nikita did not believe Gina was pregnant knocking her down and slicing her open to see if she was, Gina was empty. With the rage left in Nikita she went to find KT and killed him, hacking off his head and placing it in a bag. She knew she could not stay here any longer and fled along with the baby and took a boat at night on the river Thames and all she muttered was her and KT are going to be together forever and be a happy family. Until this day legend has it that every valentine's day when the clock strikes twelve you can see a woman paddling away with the sound of a baby's cry in the distance.

For the streets

"You pathetic girl, can't you get anything right?"

"No one will take you".

"You fucking bitch!".

"Might as well give up now".

"You were born on the streets, and you'll die on the streets."

"Once from the streets, there's no going back".

This was considered the norm for Emily, ever since she was a young girl abandoned by her mother who could not afford enough food for herself and a young girl to grow up on the streets of London she would have to live with different people whether that be her own family members or in the corrupted adoption system. Whoever Emily was put with she would always end up with the short straw as it would always be against her, even when she finally went to live with her grandparents at the age of 14 that was ok for a while and you would probably expect a happy ending that she is with her family, but that is not the case here. Until her grandfather came home one day with his drinking pals from the local spoons heavily drunk forcing her to do unthinkable things and since then things were never the same for Emily.

Even at college the boys from her classes would sometimes stop her during break or at the end of the day to get some favours, whenever asked by teachers if everything were ok she would just reply back with a simple yes in fear they would not believe her and avoid confrontation. Any money she would make would go straight to her grandparents who ran a little red district from the different properties they owned with the wide range of girls they had from different backgrounds and ages catering for different jobs, if they did not produce enough money to pay their rent they would have to live without any food and kicked out for the streets to deal with them.

Emily's father was a Politian who already had a family and three kids but after a drunken night with Emily's mother who at the time was working for her parents in the red district, he wanted nothing to do with her and just saw her as a mistake. Emily and her mother did try many times to meet and convince him to take them, in hope of a better life but he would always refuse even threating to take Emily when still an infant and throw her in the river Thames from above Tower bridge or throwing her into the adoption system in another country far away to never be seen again.

Emily had been living this type of lifestyle for as long as she could remember and had to balance doing her GCSE's and BTEC's alongside, some late nights from college one of her grandparents would collect and make her have to work the late-night job of working in the red-light district until early in the morning. She would come across all types of people in London and a few times would have to travel to other cities depending on if one of the properties were short on people making money and ensuring customers were always happy with their service.

"Did you get todays pay"?

"How much did you make today"?

"How many customers?"

"You won't be getting any food until you bring in more money"

"You stupid bitch!".

"You're lucky to be our own blood otherwise you would have been out ages ago".

As soon as Emily would return early in the morning or from doing her late-night job these were the type of questions her grandparents would ask or reply with, never satisfied, constantly money hungry to build a corrupt little empire which looked like it was being done legally but majority of the money made was dirty good money.

One day Emily's grandfather dropped her and a few other girls around town in his red Kia so they could start their daily earnings, Emily and another girl headed for the Tesco car park sitting near the bottom entrance where customer go up to do their shopping on the main shopping floor, with an empty costa coffee cup as a disguise encase Tesco staff or police see her and ask her to move away from the premises. The car park smelt obnoxious with certain areas being coated in urine, pigeons flocking to grab any food scattered on the floor and mice nibbling on anything they could find.

A few people would drop her a few loose pennies while her companion would go behind or inside some of the cars with those she would catch with her sweet eyes.

"Any spare change?"

She would ask those while they walked pass, a few were kind enough to drop her some coins, she even thought about maybe using the coins she was getting to help rebuild a better life, to have a better future away from all of this madness she was born into as it is something no one would want to experience. Emily failed to get any customers and barley managed to make even £1, before getting into the vehicle her grandad's assistant asked Emily and the other girls for today's pay. She handed him the few coins in the cup and dumped it into his hand, the look on his face could already tell you what would happen when they get home.

Once they arrived home they all got out of the car one by one heading through the front door with the assistant grabbing Emily tightly by the hand and taking her straight to her grandparents. The other girls would also live in the same house or around in one of the other properties owned by her grandparents doing drugs and other activities in the red district. Emily and the assistant charged into the dining room her grandparents were in with their accountant to see how much money they made this month.

"How much today?" they asked in anticipation.

"More than last month" he said.

You could see the delightful evil look in her grandparent's eyes as you could see great British pound signs in both of their eyes, all they needed was the kaching sound you normally see in cartoons, and a swimming pool stuffed with their earnings. All the celebrating as if they had won the world cup would have to pause, as they had another issue to deal with as Emily and the assistant had come through with him standing in the doorway throwing her to her knees.

"She's failed to bring in enough"

Her grandmother getting up from her seat limped over pulling her long hair and whacked her like a chef preparing pizza in the kitchen, Emily pleaded for her to stop but she would just keep going until her grandfather got involved and stopped her from doing any further damage.

With an ocean of tears tumbling down her face she got up from the floor, pushing pass her grandad and ran to her room, it was a small simple room that contained the ordinary things you expect to find: a wardrobe, desk, and a single bed. She did not have many things and had a phone she would sometimes have to hand over to her grandparents to ensure she did not tell anyone about their operations, hence why she would have to hide the fact that she had a boyfriend by sometimes deleting his number or changing his name to something they would not be suspicious about the same would go for the very few friends she had. Despite the fact that she had a boyfriend it did not change how he would treat her, he would just keep blaming her for things that were his own mistake, even went as far to sometimes cheat on her saying it was her own fault always using the excuse 'it is because you are from the streets'. She would even refuse to break up with him encase he would tell her grandparents something and they would think whatever someone else says is true instead of hearing her side of the story. She would even receive text messages or phone calls from customers who she would sometimes speak to or who wanted her services.

Gazing across the room from her bed to where her secret pet clownfish was behind the piled up clothes and desk, Emily went over pushing the clothes aside to feed it. Here you go little buddy unlike me at least you won't have to go hungry she thought to herself dropping a few fish flakes into the crystal fishbowl as she wiped away the tears from her mournful face. She dreamed of being in a happy family and living a normal life like those around her as she would not have to do some of the things she has done, sometimes even wondering why she had to be born into this business. The next morning, Emily woke up with a leak coming through the roof of her bedroom, pushed her fishbowl away out of sight and went straight to college without having anything to eat, managing to take a few nibbles from the apple from one of the neighbour's apple tree.

While on her way home from college Emily made a stop at the Tesco carpark she previously camped at to start her day job, perhaps this time she could earn her money with it coming to summer and more people being around. Jogging over to the bin drowning in waste, she picked up one of the costa coffee cups that weren't drenched in coffee or any other substance and used that to help with getting some money. This time she managed to get a bit more money than what she did last time, with one of the employees sorting out the trollies, so they weren't all on the main shopping floor she had to be careful otherwise he'll ask her to leave the premises. Whenever Emily would spot him she would give him a smile and say she's not causing any issues which was partially true despite how she was dressed like a chav that would start fights.

Coming down from the main shopping floor and to the carpark to unload his shopping, Mason came across Emily sitting near the bin with the entrance to get a trolley and go upstairs, she would ask people for money or any loose change they had when they would walk pass, saying cheers like a chav to those that gave her whatever they were carrying on them. As he walked passed she was still begging people for money in her chavy clothes, once done with unloading he took the trolly back looked her in the eyes and gave her the £1 coin. Emily was surprised he gave her some money and asked him a simple question.

"Heads or Tails?" she asked.

"Heads". He said, while walking off to get back into his car.

"You're lucky" she replied.

He thought to himself he defiantly must be for him to predict it right unless she was being sarcastic and saying he was lucky meant he was going to be stabbed to death in a Tesco car park if it was tails. Mason was an investor at the London stock exchange one of the biggest market exchanges in the world with many trades coming in Monday-

Friday and lived just in Battersea coming from a middleclass up bringing not a posh lifestyle like many others. Mason would see Emily in the carpark or somewhere within the area, getting out or into different cars, he found it a bit strange that she would be in the area begging for money, going to all these different houses and cars, perhaps she was popular or even a cleaner that cleans different things.

On his way to work one morning he saw Emily leaving from one of the houses on his street and again during his lunch break near Starbucks in an alleyway with a guy older than her. He found it very strange and carefully went to see what was going on, the air filled with an obnoxious smell of burning and sounds of something spitting, she was doing drugs and a few other things with the guy. Before they could notice Mason turned around but had ran into one guy from behind wearing a hoodie and a mask.

"Customer or part of the police?". He said with one hand slowly moving towards his pocket.

"Neither I was just on a walk".

The man looked Mason up and down, asking him to take off his jacket and empty his pockets.

Before Mason could hand over his belongings two undercover officers came passing through asking what was going on, with both men making a run for it and leaving on their mopeds. The officers asked if he knew what was happening and to describe the two thugs, they were going to take Emily down to the station as she seemed to be acting weird and putting her skirt back on but refused to go with them or go to the hospital nearby to get the marks on her face and arms checked. Instead, Mason insisted he would take her home, telling his boss he would need to leave early as something came up and asked Emily where she lived. Emily was hesitant at first but eventually told him as she knew what was going to happen once she got home. To avoid the awkward silence in the car he tried to engage with Emily, all he could see was her silky hair as she was looking out the window annoyed at herself.

"I keep seeing you around here, always asking for money". Said Mason.

"Are you a stalker or something?". She gave him the dirtiest look.

As she could see they were close by, she got out of his car, slamming the car door furiously any harder and she could've broken the side mirror. Her grandfather coming out the front door to throw away some old papers, saw her coming up the road.

"You know that she's been begging for money, going in and out of different houses and cars". Said Mason.

"Mind your own business, were an honest hard working family!" said her grandfather.

Shoving Emily to go inside as he followed slowly behind. Emily herself knew what her grandfather said wasn't true as the things they did behind the scenes and what she would have to do wasn't an honest way to live.

"You've been booked for a 23:00 pm and never get caught like that again otherwise it will be no food for 3 months and living in the basement with the rats". Said Emily's grandfather.

As he went into the living room to watch match of the day with a few of his pub mates. Emily went upstairs to her room and did her usual routine when she would have to meet customers, packing her bag with different clothes, making sure she completed her assignments before heading off and giving whatever money she's made to her grandparents, taking different pictures for the thirsty boys on Snapchat and Instagram and with that she was off to her customer and other potentials for the evening.

Once they went inside the house Mason drove off thinking to himself, he had to somehow help her as it didn't seem right. While driving he got a text message from one of his friends about a party and asked if he wanted to come, he pulled over to the side and replied he would come. At the party people were dancing as if they were in Ibiza with a variety of food, drinks, and girls everywhere it was similar to the scene in the great Gatsby, with the whole building just partying, a few girls caught Mason's attention, but he mainly wanted to party and see where his friend was. As the night grew older, people were starting to leave to avoid a possible noise complaint or get caught in the wrong crowd, with the numbers dropping he finally saw his friend sitting on the stretched sofa by the big fish tank.

"I've been getting with this young girl, she's quite hot and does a lot of unthinkable things, here take a look for yourself". He said.

He looked at the business card and snaps his friend would get from the girl on snapchat and realised it was the girl from the other day, not only was she doing drugs but a red light district worker too as she would sometimes record things and send it to people. Mason was quite shocked and told his friend how he's seen her around the city.

"She's quite popular among people, to tie her down will be hard". Said his friend.

Mason took a copy of the business card and searched for her different socials to see what she would post, she was only two years younger and needed to think of a way to meet her.

As days went on, once Emily came through the front door from helping her grandma from doing the shopping her grandfather on the phone called for her.

Did she get less money again?

Was she going to be kicked out?

"You have a booking at 20:00pm, from the sounds of it two rich politician so make sure you look good for them and earn some more money this time or else" said her grandfather.

Emily did her routine for exclusive customers again, packing her bag with different clothes, making sure she completed her assignments for college before heading off and giving whatever money she's made to her grandparents, taking a few pictures for the thirsty boys on Snapchat and Instagram who would flood her dms and with that she was off to the customers house, her boyfriend drove her there and as they arrived she took everything with her, giving him a forced kiss and rang the doorbell awaiting for someone to answer.

Eventually the two big white and gold doors opened, and the old man guided her inside to which she saw two familiar faces Mason's and his friend.

"For two people it's usually more but I'll do it for less" said Emily.

"We actually called to help you". Said Mason's friend Mark.

"Why do you want to help me?" said Emily

"This isn't the type of life you should be living". said Mason.

"I don't know about that". Said Mason's friend.

Mason didn't like what his friend had said and slapped the back of his head.

"I want my money and never call for me again". Said Emily.

Packing her things away and texting her boyfriend Tom to come and pick her up. Before leaving she took the money she was promised and left without another word.

"That's my money gone for nothing you owe me". Said Mason's friend.

"You can regain that with extra just invest in Tesla next week". Said Mason.

Mason was disappointed he couldn't convince Emily to stop working in the red light district and his friend wasn't helping as he was just full of lust. He would need to somehow arrange to meet her again and help her escape this red light life before it's too late. She got back into the car with the money, her boyfriend slapping her on the face annoyed that he had to drive back to get her and miss the football game that was on. On the long journey home, Emily wondered to herself why would he want to help her, he hardly even knows her or anything she's gone through they have only seen each other a few times in the city and at the house just now, once they reached home Emily told her grandfather not to take any other request from the number that wanted her so she could avoid running into Mason and his friend again.

"You have a booking 3 week from now at 17:30pm, another politician keep this up and you'll be able to take over this business from me and your grandmother". Said her grandfather smoking a fag while reading a newspaper.

As the weeks went by Mason would still see Emily around the city but would avoid her, even when he would see her on the streets or in a carpark begging for money she would avoid him and return the coin he gave her or give it to another beggar close by. The date for her other customer was coming up and so were her exams, she needed to make sure she was completely focused in order for her to get into uni. With her revision session at college slightly overrunning she only had a short amount of time to get home, shower and dressed for her exclusive customer. Her grandfather's assistant drove her and while in the back of the car she took a few pictures to upload onto her different social platforms, when they finally arrived at the destination she grabbed her bag and got out of the car heading up the stairs and ringing the doorbell.

"It's open". said the voice.

Emily found it a bit weird that the front door was opened and saw a women thinking perhaps this time her customer was a women which would be different to what she has been doing recently. But the women was dressed as a maid and simply told her that she must be here for the master of the house guiding her even further into the house. Different paintings and artwork could be seen and a few pictures of an old man with his family, she was starting to think perhaps it was someone older but once she finally reached the end of the corridor with the door slightly opened she saw who her customer was. It was Mason.

"Now I know you don't want to see me but let me help you" he said, trying to ensure her that he wasn't going to do anything.

"Why do you want to help me so much?"

"Uh, you're a stalker and if you continue I'm going to tell the police". she said.

"Look all I'm trying to do is help you" said Mason.

"It isn't that easy for me". Emily said while bursting into tears.

Mason explained how his older sister would do the same thing to help with university expenses, the amount of debt she got into by buying luxury goods and other things, but when she really needed help everyone in the family turned their backs on her as she was the disappointment of the family which ended up in her taking her own life and being wanted by many people good and bad. Emily could see why Mason would want to help her, but he was still a stranger to her, and they weren't even family. Nor has anyone ever wanted to help and care for her like this before.

Was he pretending to be the kind guy who cared?

Someone who would end up using her?

Secretly working for her grandparents. Which would explain why she would always see him around in the city at different places.

Emily had two clear choices either she could walk away and report Mason for potentially stalking her or take his offer to help her live in a better world, she didn't really know what to choose and he didn't seem like a threat either, but if he could really offer her a better life she would do it. A few days a week every month when Emily would finish with college she would go to Mason's house to learn how she could live a normal life and how to actually act when around people along with stopping her drug addition, his attraction for her growing as he got to see a different side to her.

One scorching evening while Emily was heading to Mason's house, she could feel hawk eyes following her every move, even looking over both shoulders around each street corner she took to see if someone were following her to make it easier to spot, but no one was there, all the cars were driving at a normal speed with none of them driving oddly. It made Emily wary causing her to take a longer route to Mason's house, grabbing a few snacks from the local Tesco and giving her fellow workers begging for money some lose change. She would keep a copy of Mason's house keys hidden from her grandparents and the others within the house by keeping it with her clownfish, she grabbed the keys from her back pocket, opened the door, wiped her feet, and walked inside the house.

As Emily entered the house she walked to the kitchen to get herself a drink and saw a lot of flowers around the house, she thought perhaps as it was becoming summer Mason was trying to make the house look more charming or perhaps his gardener and decorator were trying to brighten the house. In the living room she found a few more bouquet of flowers and a note saying it was for her, it put a smile on her face, smelling every bouquet in sight reminded her of a garden full of different flowers from a past dream she had. Emily sat down, waiting for Mason, he finally came into the house and could see Emily liked the flowers that were scattered around the house not just to make the house brighter but for her too. He sat next to her, with today's lesson to help with her maths work for the upcoming maths exam, as they spent more time with each other he could smell a whiff of her perfume, he couldn't hold it in any longer he was going to make a move, moving in closer for a kiss and kissing her on her enchanting peachy lips.

Emily was in shock and knew she should probably stop as she had her boyfriend, but Mason would treat her better than him and everyone she's come across, would it really be that bad?

With the two of them making out Emily's guilt for her boyfriend was starting to get to her, before she could force Mason off of her they could hear someone knocking on the door very furiously, ringing the doorbell continuously. Mason went to see who was at the door. As he opened the door he could see it was Emily's boyfriend Tom, pushing Mason to the side and launching one punch at his face to make him fall over in the doorway. Rushing around the house throwing anything in sight on the ground looking for Emily, when he finally found her he told Emily to pack her things as he was taking her back home to her grandparents. Emily refused to leave with Tom and wanted to stay which was getting on his nerves, causing Tom to flip as he threw her bouquet of flowers out the window smashing the glass into icicles and on the floor stamping on them, forcibly grabbing Emily by her hair and hands to leave with him.

Before they left Tom kicked Mason a few times in the chest and exchanged a few death threats if he saw him with Emily again, Emily pleaded with him to stop as Mason had done nothing wrong but if she were to tell Tom he had kiss her he would probably kill him. Mason holding his face and body in pain, got up from the floor, trying to run after Emily and her boyfriend, but they had already drove down the road over the speed limit. Mason rushed back to the house to get his keys driving after them, he could see they were taking the long route to her grandparents' house and followed them there. With tears rolling down Emily's face and being dragged by Tom, many neighbours could see something was about to go down, some rushing back inside to secretly observe from their windows whilst others watched on from their properties. When Mason arrived on the scene it was already too late as Emily's grandfather was also there, with Tom debriefing him on what had happened. Tom walked off with a smirk on his face, barging into Mason as if to send him a signal that he had won and no matter what happens Emily will always be with him.

"Why would you want her, she's useless!". Said her grandfather.

"She's not useless! She has potential and it's not in this industry you're working in". Shouted Mason

"You can't keep her locked up like this forever". said Mason.

"I can just watch me, you and the rest won't see her again". Said her grandfather, grabbing Emily's hand in disappoint and heading up the stairs to the house

"What is it going to take for her to be free". Said Mason.

Her grandfather paused, turning himself around to look at Mason taking a few seconds to think of his next response. Emily to be free? As long as he's alive he thought to himself that would never happen.

"You seem smart from one businessman to another you figure it out, I'll give you 4-6 months". He said.

"For the rest of you move on the shows over, thanks for coming". He said.

Everyone went back inside their houses, those who just happened to be walking through while the drama was happening, carried on walking muttering to themselves or to the neighbours close by to what they had just witnessed. Mason drove home, thinking to himself he knew what her grandfather wanted but how quickly he could get the money to ensure Emily's freedom, it would be difficult as he was only a junior apprentice trader. When he finally reached home he saw his house was still in the same state he left it in, the living room windows still smashed and police now on the scene, he explained to them it was just an argument, but they still took statements from people who saw what had happened and looked at their CCTV camera footage of the street to see what happened, even referring him to go see a doctor to get the mark on his face and body checked. Any ruined flowers he thew away and the ones that managed to survive bundled together, keeping a few of them in the kitchen and living room, he also made a few phone calls to get the windows and other things around the place fixed otherwise whenever someone would walk past his house they would think it's a perfect opportunity to go treasure hunting.

Meanwhile back at Emily's grandparent's house they were discussing with their associates and connections what they were going to do with her as they locked Emily in her room and closed her windows and doors to reduce contact with the outside world and any attempt of her escaping. She wasn't allowed to go out by herself anymore, to ensure she did not go to see Mason she had to report to someone where she was going, for how long and when she would be back. Sometimes with some of the henchmen going with her and coming back to make any possible escape futile. Even her friends from college and within the district who would want to see her would be turned down and told she was sick or not at home. The other girls who worked for her grandparents were starting to get jealous and annoyed with Emily, with all the attention she would get as even some of their customers would ask them about Emily and if they could get her instead of them, which annoyed a lot of the girls working in the district. Causing them to cut Emily's hair but luckily they didn't cut it completely off as they originally planned to teach her a lesson as the assistant stopped them in their tracks when he had come up to give Emily her food, they made her long luxurious hair short making it look like a weirdly cut fringe.

Many months passed where Emily was treated like a prisoner in very extreme conditions restricted food and contact with anyone, some days making her want to go back to her old habits. But she knew if she were to go back to her old habits then all the progress she's made since then would all be for nothing. Sometimes wondering when Mason would come to rescue her and fulfil the promise he made of having a better life, with some nights she would doubt everything that has happened thinking none of it actually happened and was all just a dream, she never actually met someone called Mason, but the marks on her body and mini photo she kept attached on her fishbowl of her and Mason ensured her every day that he was real not a figment of her imagination.

Tensions were getting very high in the properties the grandparents owned with some of the girls refusing to work, quitting, or switching to another red light district. To avoid losing so much money her grandparents had to make a choice either they pack their things and relocate their business to somewhere like Manchester, Brighton, or Leicester, or they dispose of Emily which would save their business and bring back the top girls they had back in their dirty business. It was very tempting for her grandparents to get rid of her as it would resolve so many of the problems they have had to face since taking Emily in at a young age, but with many people already suspicious of them and a few undercover cars outside watching their every move, they would need to plan their next move very carefully as killing Emily would just be the key problems resolved, what would still remain is having to deal with the police and others involved. They could even screw Mason over, not release Emily and walk away with his money, starting a new life and reconstructing the business in America, more girls equals more profit is what her grandfather thought.

It took quite a while for Mason to gather the money to ensure Emily's freedom from her greedy grandparents, once he finally got all the money he placed it in a briefcase he brought from louis Vuitton and travelled to Emily's house. He just hoped that her grandfather would keep to his word, and he could reach the house within the timeframe he agreed. With a lot of traffic around the area and the side roads closed off he wasn't going to make it in time, he thought about abandoning his car and just moving on foot but then his car would be blocking the path of the other road users. Whenever a gap would open he forced his way through the cattle of other cars, driving through as if he were in a maze trying to reach the exit, once close to the traffic light he waited for it to turn green and rushed to beat the remaining time he had left as he didn't have that much time left on the clock.

Mason just seconds away, could just see Emily's house in the distance as the second floor of the house and its roof was poking out over the hedges in front of him, with pedestrians in the middle of the road blocking him from turning his vehicle into Emily's road as they were taking part in a parade he had missed his deadline. He pulled his car to the side devastated that he didn't make it in time all because of the pedestrians that were blocking his path, when Mason went to check his phone for any messages he saw he still had 1 minute left on the clock, rushing to get his seat belt off he grabbed the bag filled with money from the back seat and ran down the road, he was going to save Emily and this time determined to make it permanent, pushing past those walking in the street as he grew ever so near to the house now, coming out of the house with movers were Emily's grandparents and other people. Mason scouted the area looking for Emily, he couldn't see her in sight but confronted her grandfather.

"Where's Emily!!". He shouted.

"The deal is off, you didn't come within the duration I gave you". Said her grandfather

Mason took his phone out to recheck the time, he was on time.

"What are you on about I'm on time". Said Mason.

He was starting to think perhaps her grandfather was trying to cheat him out of money and freeing Emily.

"Fine give me the money and I'll tell you where Emily is". He said.

Mason was skeptical whether he should hand over the money filled bag or demand to see Emily first before handing it over, but he didn't want to waste anymore time and get Emily as far away as possible. Mason threw the bag to Emily's grandfather, he opened the bag checking how much money was in the bag to make sure he wasn't being tricked and ensuring every note was real with the queen's face.

"Here's the key to her room she's in the attic of the house". Said her grandfather.

He grabbed the keys from her grandfather, pushing past the movers and other people coming in and out of the house, rushing upstairs to free Emily and fulfil his promise, unlocking all the locks on the door to loose and kicking the door open, he could see Emily was there in the room asleep with the duvet cover over her body and hair covering her face. He went over to the side of the bed to wake her up and pluck her a kiss, as he pushed the hair back he saw the girl he kissed wasn't Emily but someone completely different.

"Good morning, if only all my days could start like that". Said the girl as she was starting to wake up.

It startled Mason as he thought it was Emily but in fact a different girl in her bed and a completely different voice. Mason looked out the locked window, they had finished packing and were about to leave the premises, leaving their keys near the front of the house. The girl tried to make Mason come back to bed and hold him down, but he jumped passed the bed, rushing downstairs in hope he could ask her grandparents what happened to Emily as the room key they gave him was clearly not the key for her room but for someone else.

"Were off boys that's everything". Said her grandmother, ensuring they had packed everything.

They started their engines, driving down the road one by one in a single line, as Mason reached the front door he ran onto the streets attempting to run after them.

"Come back!!! Where's Emily"

"WHERE'S EMILY!!!!"

Printed in Great Britain
by Amazon